TALES
from the
SHADOWS

Five Stories by

ANNIE REED

TVp

Thunder Valley Press

Published by Thunder Valley Press
www.thundervalleypress.com
Cover illustration copyright © Sergey Gordeev | Dreamstime.com
Book & cover design copyright © 2013 Thunder Valley Press

ISBN: 0615825206
ISBN-13: 978-0615825205

CONTENTS

INTRODUCTION

Every big city has a neighborhood where it's not safe to walk alone in the daylight, much less after dark. A place where all manner of illegal substances are bought and sold, and sex is used like a weapon. A place where the crimes on the street don't hold a candle to what goes on behind closed doors and shuttered windows.

In Moretown Bay, the locals call that neighborhood The Shadows.

I started writing stories set in the fictional Pacific Northwest town of Moretown Bay a few years ago when I wrote the first Diz and Dee detective story. As I initially envisioned my fantasy detectives, they were serious police officers dealing with very serious magical crimes and criminals. It seemed like a natural. After all, I grew up reading crime fiction and watching crime shows and police procedurals on television. If someone would have added a little magic to a show like *Hill Street Blues,* I would have been in seventh heaven, as my dad used to say. It's no wonder I'm currently enjoying the heck out of *Grimm.*

However, as it turned out, Diz and Dee didn't want to be serious all the time, and their stories took on a more light-hearted tone. But since I have that soft spot in my heart for noir stories, I never forgot that Moretown Bay has a seedy underbelly. I just needed the right character to come along and tell me his story.

That character showed up when I wrote "Changeling" as an assignment for a fairytale noir anthology that didn't take off. Rory the cab driver was noir to his core, and he was such a strong character that he makes an appearance in two more of the stories in this volume, "Famous" and "Don't Touch."

I wrote "Ties That Bind" for Loren Coleman's anthology *WIZARDS, INC.,* published by Daw (2007). "Ties That Bind" delves into the world of corporate crime, only since magic's involved, the stakes in this story are much higher than simple downsizing. The fifth story in this collection is "Iris & Ivy," a tale of twin sisters, murder, and revenge.

The fine folks at Thunder Valley Press are putting together several more collections featuring my short fiction. Each collection will focus on a topic or genre, like this one. As long as Thunder Valley keeps wanting to publish these collections, I'll keep writing the stories. I hope you enjoy reading them.

—Annie Reed
Reno, Nevada
March 31, 2012

CHANGELING

The changeling reclined on her narrow bed in the squalid little room, rumpled sheets testifying to a busy night already spent on her back. Features flowed across her face, flesh moving like liquid to thin her lips, widen her brows, sharpen her chin and the delicate shells of her ears.

"This what you want, sugar?" she asked. Her waist narrowed, lean muscle flattening her naked belly. Her breasts shrank from the porn queen size they'd been when Rory picked her up on the street to something he could cup in his hand. "This what you're after?"

Most normals couldn't watch a changeling shift. Couldn't witness human features rearrange themselves and know, deep in the gut, it wasn't an illusion. The wrongness of it hurt the eyes, made the stomach heave and the pavement tilt underfoot. Rory didn't have a choice. He had to watch.

The changeling hadn't turned on the overhead light when she let Rory in her room. Enough watery streetlight filtered through the sheets of rain beating against the window for Rory to see her try to become what he wanted. What he'd told her was his fantasy.

A half-full World's Best Mom mug sat on the bedside table next to an overflowing ashtray. Lipstick smears circled the rim. In the dim light, the lipstick looked black. Judging by the boozy smell, the mug hadn't seen coffee in a long time.

"You got a kid?" he asked. No toys littered the room, but that didn't mean anything. Not every mother was the world's best.

She saw him looking at the mug and laughed. "Goodwill, sugar. Got it cheap. Someone's momma didn't want it no more." She took a drink. "You want some? I got a clean glass and a bottle in the closet. Five bucks extra."

The place stank of sweat and cigarettes and sex. "No." A drink wasn't what he was after.

He leaned one shoulder against the wall at the foot of her bed. Unzipped his coat. She didn't have a kid. He couldn't stay if she had a kid. He allowed himself to hope. Maybe she'd be the one.

"So?" She gestured at her face. At her reshaped body. "How'd I do?"

Close, but close wasn't good enough. "The chin's wrong," Rory said. "A dimple, right here." He touched the middle of his own chin. "Like I told you."

"Like this?" A cleft appeared in the middle of her chin, but too high up. It looked like a piercing gone wrong.

"I said here." He touched his own chin again. What was so difficult about a cleft chin? Why couldn't she get it right?

"Would be easier if you brought a picture with you," she said. "Don't you have a pic—"

"Just do what I tell you, and you won't need a damn picture."

Now he did want a drink. Frustration did that to him, but he'd quit drinking just when any other man would have started.

Rory didn't need to be reminded that he'd destroyed every picture he had. Smashed the camera and computer, snapped the backup disks in half and hurled the whole mess into the sullen gray water of the bay while the rain beat down on his bare head. By the time he'd snapped out of his rage and pain and realized what he'd done, it had been too late.

He told himself it didn't matter. Every time he closed his eyes, he could still see his wife. Saw the tenderness of her smile. Heard the music of her laugh. Felt her cool breath against his face as she leaned in to kiss him.

When he kept his eyes closed too long, he saw the dark stain of her blood, black as the lipstick on the mug. In his memory, her blood was always black, and the stench of it filled his head and left him shaky and hollow, angry and aching and so damn alone he couldn't stand it.

The new cleft in the changeling's chin was too deep. Her voice was scratchy from the booze and cigarettes, her eyes dark smudges that could have been any color at all, not his wife's clear blue, and it was all wrong, wrong, wrong.

Why couldn't any of them get this right?

The changeling's face shifted again, but Rory had had enough for one night.

"Stop," he said. "Just fucking stop."

He zipped up his coat. His wife used to wear it when the wind blew a storm in from the ocean beyond the bay to drench the city streets with rain and wind and fury, and the hood still smelled like her.

"No. Wait, sugar. I can do this. Be who you want." The changeling sat up, put her hand on Rory's arm. Gave him a seductive smile. No one wants a paying customer to walk and take his money with him. "It's what I do. Be your fantasy girl."

Rory shook her off. He made no move for the folded up bills she'd stuffed under her mattress.

When the changeling realized he didn't want his money back, she relaxed back on the bed. Her smile had a touch of cruelty to it.

"So I don't float your boat, sugar? Maybe it's not a fantasy girl you want after all."

She shifted into a lithe young man, slender hips and delicate features, and laughed at him.

Rory ignored her and let himself out. Laughter trailed behind him.

She lied. They all lied. None of them could be the person he wanted.

That didn't stop him from trying.

Rory drove a cab six nights a week. The boss didn't like him much, said he had an attitude problem, but Rory didn't care.

He was one of a handful of drivers who'd venture into the dockside neighborhoods on the east side of the bay after midnight, and the only normal at that, but Rory knew how to take care of himself. If his size and attitude intimidated his fares, he didn't much care about that either.

The cops called Moretown Bay's dockside neighborhoods "South of 40th." The locals called it The Shadows. Anything illegal with a magical bent could be bought or sold in The Shadows. Drug deals and prostitution and territory skirmishes among the goblin gangs were just the public face of waterfront crime. Much worse happened in private inside boarded-up brick buildings and behind closed doors.

Rory cruised the streets, only half looking for fares. After midnight, the wind off the bay was too cold and the possibility of facing something that could steal your soul with a spell or cleave your head from your body with a flick of a finger was too real for normals who lived uptown in their well-lit glass and steel high rises. In the light, they could reassure themselves the cops really had every magic user under control. In The Shadows, control was an illusion.

He pulled to the curb in front Snow's Palace, a strip club owned by a former vice cop—a dwarf himself—with a twisted sense of humor. From what

Rory heard, the owner always had at least one creamy-skinned, ruby-cheeked stripper working the pole. Rory had never been inside the place himself. What he wanted, he could find on the streets.

He had his eye on a group of young men clustered under the awning over the club's front door. Frat boys by the look of them. Good shoes, good clothes, maybe good tippers. If he got a half-decent fare, he could take himself off duty for the rest of the night and cruise where he wanted.

The back passenger door opened on the street side. Rory looked in the rearview mirror. Not the college boys, but a working girl, all bleach blonde hair and big tits stuffed into an outfit too small to hold them in. A swollen bruise discolored one cheekbone, the skin split in the center.

"Drive," she said.

He tried not to let his annoyance show. Working girls didn't tip. "Where?"

She gave him an address nearly a mile away. Outside The Shadows. Not where she took her tricks then.

"You off for the night?" he asked.

She glared at him in the mirror. "What's it to you?"

Nothing. It meant nothing at all, and Rory let it drop.

He drove the next couple of minutes with only the sound of his tires on wet pavement and the slap/thump of the windshield wipers breaking the silence in the cab. Traffic picked up once he crossed 40th going north. He nearly got clipped by a Lexus when the driver cut him off, and he had to slam on the brakes.

When he glanced in the rear view mirror to make sure his passenger was all right, the bruise and the cut on her face were gone.

"Pretty high rent address we're going to for a changeling working The Shadows," he said.

She settled herself into the far corner of the seat and leaned to one side. Even though Rory couldn't see all of her given the cab's barrier between the front and back seats, he knew she'd crossed her legs.

"I'm a pretty high rent girl," she said.

Rory snorted. "And I'm the Pope."

"I've got a special talent."

He knew what she'd say next.

Her voice dropped half an octave and took on a sultry, indulgent tone. "I can be anyone. Anyone at all."

"Right." He'd heard that before, over and over and over again.

She leaned forward, and Rory found himself staring into his own tired eyes in the rearview mirror.

"Even you," she said in his voice.

It was like looking at his own reflection, right down to the nose he'd broken twice in the ring and the jagged scar on his left temple, and she'd done it in an instant.

Just as quick, she shifted to a more subdued version of the woman who'd climbed into cab. She relaxed back into her corner with a self-satisfied grin.

Rory nearly forgot he was driving. Could she be the one to finally get it right?

A blaring horn brought him back to reality, and he jerked the cab back into his own lane. The changeling laughed, but it wasn't a cruel laugh. She must use that trick a lot. Must know how men would react.

"You are good, I'll give you that." Rory waited a beat. "How much?"

"That one was for free. You can't afford the real thing."

"How would you know?"

She made a gesture at the dingy interior of the cab. "Low rent."

"That's the cab, not me, sweetheart." He forced himself to smile at her. "Tell me how much."

She did. It wasn't a ridiculously high amount, something well below the price nobody but the guys who lived in luxury penthouses could afford, but high enough Rory would have to hustle fares for a couple weeks to make the rent on his own dingy walk up.

It didn't matter. Whatever the cost, he'd pay it.

"You've got yourself a deal," he said. "Where?"

He watched her think about it. Back to wherever she did business in The Shadows, or was she the kind of girl who'd take a cabbie to her own home for a quick morph and fuck?

She finally gave him a new address in a working class district. Just how many homes did she have, anyway?

He found a place to park half a block away from her place and opened the back door of the cab for her like he was on a damn date. The woman who climbed out looked college age. Her hair was long and dark now, her makeup minimal.

She needed two keys to get into her apartment, one for the lobby and one for the apartment door. Inside, her place was neat and tidy. Framed black and white portraits of trees adorned the walls. A chest of drawers with a small flat screen television angled on top was against one wall, a well-used sofa with over-stuffed cushions took up most of another. He half expected a cat to saunter out from the bedroom to greet him.

"I didn't steal this," she said, gesturing at the room. "In case you're wondering."

Some changelings didn't just copy appearances.

They stole lives. Changed themselves into a real person and took over that person's life. More than broken backup disks and memories were buried in the gray water of the bay.

"That's good to know," Rory said.

Not that he believed her, but he was safe. No one would want his life. Most days he didn't either.

"Money," she said, and pointed to the chest of drawers. "Put it there, or you get out now."

He peeled off almost all the hundreds he kept in a roll in his pocket. He saw her eye the remaining money, what little there was.

"You're a man of your word," she said.

"Don't sound so surprised."

"I am. The Shadows don't attract honorable men."

Or women? He put the money in front of her television. "We have a deal?"

She nodded and switched off all the lights in the apartment save for one dim lamp tucked away behind one end of the sofa. "Tell me what you want."

Rory did. He told this stranger about the way his

wife's eyes burned icy blue when the moon was full, how her skin warmed beneath his touch. How she'd come to him in a thought before he'd ever seen her in person, and how he knew, the first time he tasted her, that he was lost.

He described not only her body but who she was to him. He told this changeling more than he'd ever told anyone else. More, but not all. Never all. The rest of it he couldn't even tell to himself.

When he finished, the changeling's body shifted. Her skin lightened, and her ears grew delicate tips. Her lips thinned, her nose turned aquiline, her chin sharpened and a cleft dented inward at the precise spot it needed to be. Her eyes morphed into a clear, icy blue, her fingernails into blunted weapons.

"How did you do that?" Rory barely breathed the question, so afraid he'd break the spell.

"I have a special talent," the changeling said in his wife's melodious voice.

Rory had to clear his throat before he could speak again. "How long do I have?" A minute? An hour? Half a lifetime?

"Long enough." She held out her hand. "Is this what you wanted?"

Rory took his wife's hand and followed her into the bedroom.

Some part of his mind understood the changeling wasn't his wife, but his body didn't care. He'd been so lonely for so long, and she even smelled right. By the time they were both naked, Rory had begun calling her by his murdered wife's name.

Then he saw the mark.

Low on her belly, the fairy symbol marred the smooth surface of her skin. Something taken, something left behind, but not a fair trade. Not by half.

"You didn't even ask me," he said.

"Ask you what?" his changeling wife said.

"You just went and did it like it shouldn't matter to me." Maybe to her people it didn't, but he wasn't her people. He was a normal. A human man, with human wants and needs and feelings, and she'd known that when she married him. "Why would you do something like that? Because it wouldn't have been pure? Would have been a half breed?"

Beneath him, the changeling froze, her eyes widened in alarm, the blue leeching out the edges. But the old rage had a grip on Rory now and he barely noticed.

"Or just because it was mine?"

Rory's voice was as cold as steel. The changeling tried to push him off, but he'd always been too big and strong for his wife to push around, even with the strength that her people's particular brand of magic gave her. The changeling must have realized that. She started to shift into something else, something with enough strength and the right shape to fight back.

"No!" Rory's hands wrapped around her neck. "Don't you leave me. Not yet. I'm not done with you. I need to know why. You never told me why!"

The changeling clawed at his arms. Rory didn't even feel it. One of her hands flailed at his face, reopening the old scar on his temple. Blood dripped onto the navy blue pillow beneath her head, red drops turning black on the dark fabric.

The rage took him then. The same rage he'd channeled when he was younger that let him pummel opponents twice his size in the ring no matter how much abuse his body took.

The same rage he'd felt the night his wife told him she'd let the fairies take their unborn child.

When Rory came back to himself, the changeling was dead and he was sitting naked on the side of the bed, his arms trembling. The hollow ache inside him burned as fresh and raw as the scar on his face that still dripped blood.

She'd never told him why. All this time he'd thought he just wanted more time with his dead wife, but what he really wanted was the answer she'd never given him.

He covered the changeling's half-morphed face with the blood-spotted pillowcase and wrapped her in her bed sheets. He cleaned up the few spots of his blood on the carpet, then searched through her apartment for any sign she had children of her own. He doubted it. He refused to believe that any woman who'd ever held her own child in her arms would be so cavalier about a fairy mark over her womb.

He found nothing in the apartment but overdue bills and rancid food in the refrigerator. No one had lived in this apartment for a long time. The changeling wouldn't be missed.

Rory had a bad moment when he carried her out the front door. He thought he saw something lurking in the shadows. Something with sharp teeth and sharp ears, and a hunger for children not its own.

"You already got your piece of me," he said. "I've got nothing left to give."

The words *"foolish man"* drifted to him on a sudden breeze, and then the presence was gone. He dumped the changeling in the trunk, and when he shut the lid, rain started to fall.

Rory knew his way around The Shadows. He knew which docks were claimed by the goblin gangs and which were open territory. He knew whose boat he could take and when they'd be back looking to use it for their own business. He knew the currents and the tides and the perfect place to dump the body. He'd done it all before.

The gray water of the bay gleamed black at night. It swallowed the changeling fast, and then Rory was alone in the rain with nothing but his thoughts for company.

He'd spent months looking for someone like this changeling. She'd been special, but was she the only one? He doubted it. Somewhere out there was another changeling who could give him back his wife. Who would finally give him an answer so he could fill the void in his heart and start to heal. He just had to find her.

As many times as it might take, he'd just have to find her.

FAMOUS

The cab pulled into the loading zone in front of Kitty's Kool Kat Lounge. The pink neon sign over the entrance promised live nude dancers. Jeremy doubted they'd be totally nude, but that wasn't what he was really here for.

"Seventeen-fifty," said the cab driver.

The windshield wipers slapped a steady beat against the late night rain off the bay as Jeremy dug out two tens from his wallet. Enough for a tip, not enough to make an impression on the driver. Not enough for the man to remember he was here.

Jeremy passed the money through the slot in the clear plastic shield between the driver and the back seat. "Keep the change," he said.

The driver grunted as he took the cash. He was a bald guy twice Jeremy's age. He had a scar bisecting one eyebrow, and the kind of muscular neck Jeremy had seen on guys who worked out but never really bulked up. The driver's eyes were bloodshot, and he had enough scruff on his lined face to make him look like Bruce Willis after a three-day bender. He'd driven as if he was sober, and he'd taken Jeremy to the kind of place he wanted to go. Beyond that, Jeremy didn't care if the guy was drunk off his ass. In fact, that might make things easier in the long run.

"Let me give you a piece of advice," the driver said.

Jeremy was about ready to make a run from the cab to the club. The driver hadn't said a word to him since Jeremy caught the cab downtown and asked the guy to take him to a nightclub, any nightclub, in The Shadows.

Jeremy kept his hand on the door handle but didn't open the door. "I give you a tip and now you talk to me?" he said.

The driver looked at him in the rear view mirror. "Think you're a smart guy, don't you?"

Jeremy tensed. "What did you say to me?"

"Guys like you, you're a dime a dozen. You want to step out on the wild side, get away from your boring life in your uptown apartment with your uptown girlfriend, so you come down here to slum it up with the magic folk. You ask me to take you to a place where the cops won't bust your ass for paying a little too much attention to a girl who can look like anyone you ever had a wet dream about. Am I right?"

Jeremy felt himself flush. This guy drove a smelly, junk heap of a cab into the seamiest part of Moretown Bay, and he thought he was good enough to give someone like Jeremy advice? What a joke. But Jeremy made himself sit still and quiet and act like he was listening.

"Cops fish guys like you out of the bay all the time," the driver said. "You don't want to be one of them, so keep your eyes open and your dick in your pants. The girls down here, the ones that aren't human, they're the kind who steal more than your wallet."

Okay, enough was enough. Even a mild-mannered man would stick up for himself at this point.

"I can take care of myself," Jeremy said.

"I bet all the smart guys they fish out of the bay said that, too."

Jeremy kept himself from touching the knife he had in its special pocket in his pants. It wasn't time for the world to find out about him. He had work to do first. A reputation to build. Places to go, people to kill. A small-time loser stuck driving a cab for a living wouldn't know anything about that.

"Thanks for the advice," Jeremy said. He made himself smile and nod and pretend to be sincere.

The driver shook his head. "I'm gonna read about you in the papers, aren't I? One of the missing, or one of the dead."

Oh, you'll read about me in the papers one day, Jeremy thought as he escaped the cab. You just won't know it's me.

The inside of the nightclub was like any other

tittie bar, which was something of a disappointment.

Jeremy had moved up the coast to Moretown Bay from Portland a few weeks ago, and this was his first real excursion into The Shadows. He'd heard so many whispers about the dockside neighborhoods on the east side of the bay. The locals said this part of town was where drugs and magic and crime ruled, and the cops didn't even pretend to be in charge.

He'd built up quite a fantasy about the place in his mind. He'd expected a strip club in The Shadows, a place where magic wasn't strictly regulated, to exceed even his own outrageous fantasies. But so far all he saw were a few half-naked women dancing on a raised runway behind a U-shaped, black-topped bar. A few dozen little round tables and wooden chairs painted black were scattered around the floor. The chair backs had stylized cat eyes and whiskers in pink neon on the back, the club's logo, no doubt.

Jeremy sighed. The music was loud, the air smoky, and the drinks would be watered down and over-priced. He hoped this trip wasn't a waste.

The club's clientele was exclusively male. A

few uptown types like Jeremy, complete with sports jackets and silk polo shirts, sat at tables here and there, but most of the men were a rough sort—bikers, fishermen, wharf rats who picked up whatever work they could, and truckers who spent their days driving and their nights drinking. A couple of topless waitresses moved among the tables, clearing away empty glasses and replacing them with fresh drinks.

Jeremy took an empty seat at the crowded bar. The bartender, a topless older redhead with breasts too perfect and full to be natural, put a napkin down on the smooth surface in front of him.

"Ten bucks a drink, two drink minimum," she said. "In advance."

Jeremy took a twenty out of his wallet and put it on the bar. "Gin and tonic," he said.

The bartender looked at him. Her eyes were deep, emerald green, and she had a row of freckles across her pert nose.

Jeremy took another ten out of his wallet and laid it on the bar with the twenty. "Keep the change," he said.

She nodded at him and smiled. Her teeth were white and straight. Jeremy looked down as she took the money, and he was just in time to see her nipples contract into perfect little buds flushed deep red.

"Thanks," she said.

The guy two stools down snorted. "Great trick, Kat. Never get tired of seeing that."

The bartender rocked her shoulders, making her breasts jiggle. Her nipples flattened out, the flush gone. "Oh, you do, do you, Mort? I'll have to keep that in mind."

She left to mix Jeremy's drinks.

"What was that all about?" Jeremy asked.

"What, you ain't never seen a changeling before?" The guy took a long swig from his beer. "Trust me, kid. That ain't all they can do. You fuck a changeling once, you don't go back to vanilla pussy again."

A changeling. Jeremy had never seen one up close, at least not that he knew of.

That was the thing about changelings. They could be anyone and you'd never know, not until they died. Then they reverted back to their true forms, which Jeremy heard wasn't anything close to human.

The women Jeremy had worked with before, they were all mortals like himself, although he wasn't vanilla. Not anywhere close.

Changelings. This was exciting.

This was exactly what he was looking for.

"Are all the girls in here changelings?" he asked.

The guy snorted again. "That's why we drink this over-priced beer, kid. You wanna play, you gotta pay."

Jeremy paid closer attention to the girls dancing behind the bar. They all had perfect shapes—flat bellies, round asses, and pert, perfect breasts. Their faces were smooth, their cheeks rosy, their lips full and sensuous. They danced to music that sounded like liquid sex, all deep, throaty bass notes and smooth jazz riffs that flowed from one song to the next without ever reaching a climax.

Changelings. All he had to do was pick which one.

It had been easier with the other girls. Jeremy had a type. Dark hair, dark eyes, not too much makeup, not too aggressive a stare. He'd found his type in bars from Stockton to Sacramento, from Medford to Salem to Portland. He hadn't used his knife on all of them. Some he'd only frightened so badly that he knew they'd never turn him in to the police. He didn't worry about them. They'd only been practice, after all. Every great artist had to practice before he began work on his masterpiece.

So far the police hadn't connected the dots, but Jeremy thought that was because he'd ranged too far and wide. He intended to change all that in More-town Bay.

The place had a reputation. Too many magic users crammed into too small a part of a too-big city. Drugs and corruption went hand in hand here, and that was just among the mortal population. Add in criminal magic users, and the police were already over-worked. Jeremy figured he could build himself quite a reputation of his own. He'd be famous, and he'd move on before anyone ever caught him.

The bartender put both drinks down on the bar in front of him. Jeremy took a sip from one glass. Watered down, as he expected. That was fine. He didn't want to get drunk. He wanted to remember every detail, and he couldn't do that if he was wasted. He wanted to enjoy every minute of his first time with a changeling.

He considered whether the bartender should be the one. It had been a neat trick, what she'd done with her nipples. Jeremy didn't like redheads, but he bet they could change their hair color as easily as they could the rest of themselves. But there was something hard about her, about the way her stare was challenging, like when she hadn't picked up the twenty off the bar but waited for Jeremy to give her a tip even though she hadn't done anything to earn it. Jeremy didn't like aggressive girls.

He picked up his two drinks and wandered over to an empty table near the back. He sat down and began to watch the other girls in the club.

There were four waitresses, all topless, all as perfect in their body shapes as the dancers on stage.

Jeremy watched them as they moved among the tables, deftly avoiding being groped while they served drinks. None of them gave any of the men a lap dance. Tips went on their trays, not in the waistband of their black short-shorts with the long, kitty cat tails in the back.

At first, Jeremy thought the tails were part of the costume. Then he saw one of the waitresses laugh, and the tail of her costume curled and then relaxed.

Jeremy blinked. They actually *had* cat tails.

What would it be like to be with a woman with an actual tail?

Jeremy finished off his first drink and started in on the second. One of the waitresses approached his table. She was shorter than the rest. Her hair was dark, long enough that it touched her collar bone in front, shorter in the back. Her eyes were dark brown, her lips the kind of dusty red that had nothing to do with lipstick.

"Can I get you another round?" she asked.

Jeremy tried to see around to the back of her shorts. The need to see her tail was almost visceral.

He hadn't been this excited about something new since the first time he'd touched his knife to smooth skin and blood had welled up against the blade.

"I'm sorry," he said. "This might be rude, but could I see your tail?"

She looked at him, and he could have sworn her eyes got darker, although it could have been a trick of the low light in the bar. She swiveled her hips, and her tail curled around the side of her waist.

"This little thing?" she asked. "I almost forget I have it when I'm here."

It looked exactly like a cat's tail, sleek-furred and blunt-tipped. Jeremy had to keep himself from reaching out to touch it. He imagined that touching a waitress might get him thrown out of the bar. The bouncer at the door was twice his size, and he hadn't looked entirely human.

What she'd said about her tail sunk in. "You don't have it all the time?" he asked.

"Part of the costume." She looked over her shoulder, then turned back to him and leaned over a bit. "I can do this, too."

Jeremy watched, fascinated, as two cat ears sprouted from her head like horns, then melted back beneath her hair.

"Kat doesn't like it when we mess with the costume," she said, her voice pitched so low Jeremy had to strain to hear her over the music. "But it's kind of fun, don't you think?"

"Kat, that's the bartender?"

"Yeah. She runs the place. She's a good boss, but it's not really my thing, you know? I'm just here until I can make enough to go to school." She grinned at him. "I guess that's my pitch to get you to leave me a good tip. You don't mind, do you?"

Jeremy dug two twenties out of his wallet. His fingers brushed the knife on the way out of his pocket.

Patience, he told himself as he put the money on the table.

"Gin and tonic, right?" She picked up the money off the table and her smile got bigger. "And a really good tip. I think you're going to be my favorite customer of the night."

When she turned away to get his drinks, she put an extra sway in her hips. Her tail bounced along behind her.

Only after she'd left did Jeremy realize he'd never looked at her naked breasts.

The second round of drinks had no more effect on him than lemonade. When he made his way to the men's room to relieve his bladder, the room didn't tilt off balance like it did the few times he'd been truly drunk.

Tonight was the night, he could feel it in his bones. He was ready. His waitress was perfect. He only had to figure out how to get her alone.

As it turned out, he didn't have to. She was waiting for him in the hallway outside the men's room when he finished.

"Sshhh," she said, putting a finger to her lips. "We're definitely not supposed to do this, so don't make a sound."

She took his hand in hers and led him further down the hall, away from the bar. They passed a closed door marked "Office" and another door to the largely unused ladies' room. Beyond that was a velvet-curtained doorway opposite a door marked "Exit." The waitress pushed the velvet curtain aside and pulled Jeremy into the dark room beyond.

"Where are we?" Jeremy whispered.

"Dressing room." She clicked on a lamp that gave off about as much light as a nightlight. "We're not supposed to bring customers back here, but..." She shrugged. "You're kinda cute, and I don't think you've ever been with anyone like me before, right?"

Jeremy shook his head, content to play the naive vanilla mortal and see where this went.

"I like guys like you," she said. "Not that I do this kind of thing a lot, but I really liked that you've got a thing about my tail. That's not what guys usually want. It makes it kind of fun. Makes me feel special."

"So," Jeremy said. "Can I see it? I mean, without the costume?"

She nodded and grinned a playful kind of grin, like a kid who knew she was doing something naughty. She slid her short-shorts off, and then turned around.

He could have done it then, clamped his hand over her mouth and slid his knife into her, but the sight of her black fur-covered tail emerging from the base of her spine right over her round, naked buttocks fascinated him. The tail twitched back and forth over her creamy skin like it had a life of its own.

"Can I touch it?" he asked.

She smiled at him over her shoulder. "I was hoping you'd want to."

He reached out and stroked her tail, and she wrapped it around his arm. It was hard and ropy, as substantial as his fingers but much more expressive.

"I hope that's not all you're going to do," she said. "Just pet my tail."

It occurred to him that she was fully naked now. She bent a little at the waist, the move clearly inviting.

Jeremy unzipped and moved in behind her. The knife in his pocket was practically burning through his trousers. He was ready. He'd touched her tail.

In a minute, he'd touch her blood.

He thought the tail would get in the way, but their bodies fit together as well as every other woman Jeremy had ever been with. Her tail wrapped around his waist, thumped against his belly, stroked the side of his cheek.

He understood now what the man at the bar meant. He'd never go back to a vanilla mortal again, but not for the same reason as other men.

Jeremy slipped the knife from his pocket without missing a stroke. All the other women he'd had before were just practice for this, the first one that really counted.

She was just the right fit beneath him. He slid the knife between her ribs at an upward angle at the same time he clamped his hand over her mouth. He held her tight as she shuddered and her blood spilled out over his hand.

She was perfect.

He savored the moment until she became too heavy to hold. He laid her down gently on the floor and crouched down beside her. He shouldn't wait, but he wanted to see what she looked like in her true form. He wanted to remember every minute of his time with her, including her transformation.

When she changed, it wasn't what he'd expected. Her tail melted away, reabsorbed into her body, but instead of turning into something inhuman, her body thickened at the waist, flattened at the hips. Her breasts shrank inward, her shoulders widened. Her thighs and arms turned muscular, and her hair pulled back until it was short against her skull. Short, and dirty blonde. Just like his own.

What the hell?

She turned over on her back and looked up at him with his face.

"Surprise," she said in his voice.

He stumbled back, falling over himself in his haste to get back on his feet. She was on him in an instant.

She might have had his body, but she was inhumanly strong, much stronger than he was. She knocked his feet out from under him. He fell flat on his back, his head bouncing hard on the floor. He dropped the knife as she fell on top of him. Before he could grab for it, her arm lengthened and she snatched it away.

"One thing you should know about changelings," she said. "We can be anybody we want to be. Even you."

"But I killed you," he said.

"You tried to. That's another thing." She poked him in the chest with her finger. "Our heart's not in the same place as yours. That's the only way a human can tell we aren't. Human, that is. Maybe you should have studied up on us before you tried to kill me. We heal really fast when you don't hit us in the heart."

His own face stared down at him barely inches away from his own. He felt dizzy. If he hadn't already been flat on his back, he might have passed out.

"What do you want?" he asked.

"Your life," she said. "I told you working here wasn't really my thing. I think I want to be you for a while, see what that's like."

Be him? "You don't want my life. It's boring. Really."

"Oh, I doubt that." She grinned at him with his face. The expression had no mirth in it. "You stuck that knife in me like a pro. I'm pretty sure you've done that before. Want to know what it feels like?"

Before Jeremy could say or do anything, she'd sprouted another arm to hold him down and another to cover his mouth. He felt his own knife slip in between his ribs, angled up toward his heart.

The pain was exquisite. He shuddered as wave after wave ripped him apart with every breath.

Her eyes widened, the pupils darkening. "Oh, my. I can see why you like it. I might have to do this again."

She watched him intently as he struggled to get free, but he was getting weaker every second. Finally she dropped her hands away. He tried to scream, but he couldn't take enough air into his lungs.

She stood up. She was still naked, but her body was his again now, right down to the scar on his thigh from when he'd fallen as a child and the sparse hair on his chest. She held his wallet in hands that looked just like his. She took out his combination driver's license/identity card, the brand new one he'd gotten only weeks ago when he'd moved to the bay.

"Jeremy Jones, huh?" she said. "I think I'll like that name." She waved the license at him. "Everything I need, right here, to be you, Jeremy. How nice for the state to put it all in one convenient place."

A sound like rushing waves started to build inside Jeremy's head. The dim light from the nightlight seemed to be fading. He tried to say something, but he couldn't catch his breath.

"What was that?" she said. "Did you have some last words for me?"

Jeremy thought about all the hard work he'd done, all the practice he'd put into making himself the perfect killer. He'd even had a name picked out for himself: *Lady Killer.* If the cops hadn't picked it out for him, he'd planned on sending an anonymous note and signing it the Lady Killer.

"I was going to be famous," he murmured.

She stared down at him. Just for a moment, her

eyes turned emerald green and as hard as stone. "Oh, don't worry."

She bent over and picked up his knife. The last thing Jeremy saw was the changeling wiping his own blood off the blade.

"You will be," she said. "You will be."

IRIS & IVY

Iris leaned her weary back against the inside of the front door to her apartment. She felt as well as heard the latch snap shut.

Home again, home again, whoop de doo.

She closed her eyes and concentrated. In her mind's eye, she saw a faint green glow surround the lock. She kept concentrating until the glow spread to fill the crack between the door and the jamb, like a bit of glow-in-the-dark weather stripping.

Satisfied the bit of threshold magic would hold, she opened her eyes and pulled off the wig with its long, brassy red curls. Her scalp itched. She scoured her fingers through her own blonde hair until the skin on her head tingled.

Her face itched, too. She'd caked the makeup on pretty heavy tonight. Foundation and blush. False eyelashes so thick they looked like furry caterpillars crouching on her eyelids. Enough steel grey and dark brown eye shadow to make her look like the sexiest nearly-dead person trolling the dockside bars. She couldn't wait to wash all the crap off her face so she could get back to being herself.

Changelings shifted their appearance with hardly a second thought. All they had to do was see you, or better yet touch you, and presto chango, say hello to a brand new version of yourself, original model no longer required. Non-changelings like Iris had to work a little harder to become someone else.

"Well?" she said to the not-quite-empty apartment. "What did you think of that one?"

The wig she still held jerked out of her hand and floated in the empty air in front of her. The elastic netting that anchored all those red curls filled out.

"Oh, you're so big and tall, you man, you," said the disembodied voice in front of Iris. "Could you possibly help poor lost little old me?"

The accent was thick Southern belle, the fake kind northerners who'd never been farther south than New York City used when they wanted to make fun of someone born in a Gulf Coast state. The voice was accompanied by the overpowering scent of gardenias.

"Stop it," Iris said. "I'm trying to help you, remember? Don't make this any more difficult for both of us than it already is."

She pushed past the floating wig and stepped out of the heels that hurt her feet.

The shoes weren't hers, just like the obscenely short spaghetti strap dress wasn't hers. The wig wasn't even something she'd pick out on her own. They were all red, and red wasn't Iris's color.

None of her borrowed clothes fit her quite right, but then again, Ivy'd had some work done over the years. Iris wanted back in her comfortable jeans, in her oversized sweatshirt and the ratty tennis shoes that fit her feet like a glove. She wanted to curl up on the sofa with a glass of wine and a good book, and fall asleep right there if the mood took her.

Most of all, she wanted her apartment back all to herself, like it had been before the ghost of her dead twin took up residence.

The wig dropped to the floor. "I'm sorry," said Ivy's disembodied voice.

The fake southern accent was gone. So was the smell of Ivy's favorite perfume.

"It's hard being stuck like this," Ivy said. "You know that."

Yeah. Iris did. She felt sorry for her sister, but she'd heard the pout in her twin's voice. Funny how after so many years of growing up in the same house, she didn't actually have to see her sister to know what expression would be on her face.

"You never answered me," Iris said, ignoring Ivy's obvious ploy.

Their parents used to coddle Ivy, giving in to her every whim. Odd, considering Iris and Ivy were twins, but Iris supposed even with identical siblings, parents were bound to favor one over the other.

Not that they were identical in every way. Certainly they'd looked alike when they'd been younger, but Iris had always been the practical, reliable one. Ivy had been the wild child.

Iris used to wonder sometimes if the fates hadn't mixed them up somehow, putting the wrong consciousness into her body, or into Ivy's. Maybe somewhere out in the world there was another mismatched set of identical twins grappling with the same not quite sameness.

Ivy didn't say anything. Still hoping for sympathy, no doubt, but Iris had never coddled Ivy when she was alive. She wasn't about to start now. She needed to keep Ivy on topic. If Iris couldn't find what Ivy needed in order to move on, she might be stuck with her ghostly sister for a long, long time.

"Well?" Iris asked again. "Did I find the right guy?"

Iris's carryall slid off her shoulder and floated in the air next to the wig. The bag was Ivy's home outside of Iris's apartment. Iris didn't know why Ivy needed the bag to travel, and she wasn't about to ask.

"It was dark tonight." Ivy's pout was back.

"You don't have eyes, Ivy, remember? You told me if I took you along, you'd be able to tell."

Iris plopped down on her sofa and bent over to rub her tired feet. She'd never understood why Ivy preferred five-inch heels to comfortable shoes. The balls of Iris's feet burned from hours of walking from one trendy tourist-trap down by the waterfront to the next. The cobblestone pedestrian walkways the Moretown Bay city councilmen thought looked quaint were hell on anything other than tennis shoes or low-heeled boots.

She'd just spent five hours wandering from bar to bar, pretending to flirt with any man who appeared interested just so Ivy would have a chance to do whatever it was that ghosts did when they were trying to recognize the person who'd killed them. Dressed in Ivy's clothes and wearing a wig just like the one Ivy had worn when she died, Iris had attracted a lot of attention, but she hadn't made anyone nervous.

"He could have been the one," Ivy said.

Iris knew which guy Ivy meant. Out of all the

men who'd tried to pick Iris up, only one had given Iris a serious case of the creeps, but he hadn't acted like he'd seen the ghost of the woman he'd killed.

"Could have been." Iris pinched the bridge of her nose. "I went through all this for a 'could have been'?"

Iris had been trolling tourist bars for weeks now, looking for the man who'd killed Ivy. Her twin hadn't been all that helpful with the search. She'd probably been drunk when she was killed. The wild child had grown into quite the party girl, or at least she had been the last time Iris saw her.

As for Ivy's killer, Iris was beginning to think the man had been merely passing through. By the time the ghost of her twin had shown up late one night, nearly giving Iris a heart attack when the grisly apparition pulled the covers off while Iris was sound asleep, Ivy's murderer was no doubt already long gone on his way to new victims.

The carryall seemed to deposit itself in the over-stuffed chair opposite the sofa. Iris's apartment wasn't all that big, just a living room large enough to squeeze in a sofa and chair and a wall-mounted gas fireplace, a kitchen that felt more like a hallway than a real kitchen, and a bedroom that accommodated Iris's double bed and not much else.

Until Ivy had shown up, Iris thought the apartment was cozy. Now it felt claustrophobic.

"I need better light," Ivy said. "Not a bar surrounded by so much dark energy. I need to see him in a safe place."

A safe place. "Like here, you mean," Iris said. "You want me to invite your murderer here?"

Even if the guy wasn't the man who'd murdered her twin, the last thing Iris wanted to do was invite a creep who'd tried to slide his hand up her dress into her own apartment.

"I'll know if it's him," Ivy said. "You said you'd help me. I need you to do this. There's no one else I can ask."

That was the hell of it. Iris knew Ivy was right.

Iris had very little magic of her own, barely enough to keep her threshold energy in place and a *don't mess with me* vibe going when she needed it.

But her magic did let her do a couple of other things. Useful things, as far as her dead sister was concerned.

Most humans couldn't feel the subtle charge of magic that allowed a changeling to assume a new form. Iris could.

When her boss at Social Services sent out a caseworker to check on reports of suspected child abuse, Iris was assigned to tag along whenever the department had reason to believe a changeling was involved. Not that changelings didn't have kids of their own, but a suddenly abusive parent might be a changeling in disguise who'd killed and replaced the child's original mother or father.

Family bonds were something else Iris could identify. She could tell if a kid didn't belong to the changeling, either by blood or adoptive bond.

That family bond was what had drawn Ivy to Iris. Ivy had never set foot in Iris's apartment during life—hell, Iris couldn't even remember exactly when they'd last talked on the phone or seen each other in person—but the thin strand of magic that bound the two sisters together had drawn Ivy's ghost from the bottom of the bay where her killer had dumped her body right to Iris's bedside.

The night that Ivy first appeared was the only time she had manifested into something close to a physical presence. Ivy's body had yet to be found. Officially she was listed as missing, Iris had checked.

Ivy's body might never be found. The waters in the bay were deep and cold. Only the most power-ful—and the most expensive—wizards could hope to locate a single body at the bottom of all that murk. Neither Ivy nor the city had that kind of money to spend.

If Ivy's body looked anything like the bloated, rotted shade that had pulled the covers off Iris in the middle of the night, perhaps it was best if her sister's body stayed buried in silt. Iris still had nightmares about that night. Ivy had thankfully never appeared to Iris again.

All Iris could do to help her sister was exactly what she had been doing. But to invite a killer into her home? Could she go that far? She wasn't brave. She was practical. Practical people didn't do things that would get them killed.

"He gave you his number, didn't he?" Ivy asked from somewhere near the chair.

He had. Iris had folded up the napkin with the man's cell phone number and put it in her carryall.

"You know he did." Iris had planned to throw the napkin away.

"Call him." The ghostly voice had taken on the same stern tone their mother had used on Iris, never on Ivy.

Iris hadn't heard her mother's voice in over five years. Their parents had passed away in their sleep, victims of carbon monoxide poisoning from a faulty exhaust system in the motorhome that was supposed to take them on a meandering, cross-country journey, the first of many they planned for their retirement years.

Iris's parents had never once visited her after their deaths. They were at peace. Ivy wasn't.

Iris massaged her sore calves. It was well after

midnight. She had a meeting at eight, and a long day of home visitations after that. She wanted to curl up on the sofa and go to sleep, but Ivy would never let her sleep if she didn't promise.

"Tomorrow," Iris said. "It's too late to call to-night. I'll call him tomorrow."

The napkin with the creep's phone number seemed to pluck itself out of the carryall. It floated across the room until it settled, number side up, on the sofa next to Iris.

"Tomorrow," Ivy said.

Sudden warmth engulfed Iris. It came this time not with the overpowering odor of gardenias, but with the natural, healthy smell of the herbal shampoo their mother had washed their hair with when they'd been kids.

When they were little, their mother had bathed them together. Iris had a picture of the two of them in the tub, soap bubbles in their identically cut blonde hair, in one of the photo albums in a box at the bottom of her closet. They'd both been smiling in the picture, the kind of big, happy grins only young children can have. Children who don't know the world isn't a happy, safe place.

"I love you, sis." Ivy's voice surrounded Iris as much as the warmth of her embrace. "I don't know what I'd do without you."

Ivy was the last of Iris's family. When Ivy left to go wherever the dead went, Iris would be all alone in the world. This warmth would be gone. As irritating as Ivy could be, she was still Iris's twin. Ivy hadn't asked to be murdered.

"I love you, too," Iris said. "I always will."

The creep was all too eager to take Iris up on an offer of dinner out.

She asked him to pick her up at her apartment. She figured she could invite him in for small talk, maybe a quick drink so that Ivy could get a good look at him. Even if he wasn't the guy, Iris planned to bow out of the subsequent dinner date, claiming a sudden onset of the flu.

This time Iris toned down the foundation, blush,

and eye shadow, and left the false eyelashes off. She didn't want to put on the wig, but he thought she had long, red curls—just like the murderer thought Ivy'd had long, red curls—not the messy blonde hair Iris never bothered to style. He might not recognize her without the wig.

Iris refused to think of the creep by name. She didn't want to get to know him that well. She'd given him a fake name to go along with the fake hair. As far as he knew, her name was Roxy, she worked uptown in a boring office job, and she bar-hopped at night for a little excitement.

"You can get all the excitement you need right here," he'd said the night before, gesturing at his crotch. Subtle, he was not.

He was also five minutes early for their date. Probably for the best. Iris had worked up a major case of nerves between the time she put on her own best dress and the buzzer rang for her building. She'd given the creep her apartment number on the phone. None of the buzzers in the lobby had names below the apartment numbers. He wouldn't be able to tell that she wasn't really Roxy, the adventuresome secretary, but plain old Iris playing dress up to snare a killer.

Iris buzzed him up. She didn't know exactly where Ivy was. Her sister had been uncharacteristically silent ever since Iris got home from work. Only the faint, magical tug on the bond between them let Iris know Ivy was still there.

"Are you ready?" Iris asked while she waited for the creep to walk up the three flights of stairs. The elevator had been broken ever since Iris lived in the building.

Instead of a verbal response, Iris felt a chill in the air that vanished almost as soon as she recognized it.

"I'm nervous, too," Iris said.

She never invited anyone she didn't know well into her apartment. The threshold magic was her only barrier against anyone or anything that might mean her harm. Once she invited the creep into her apartment, she had no way to protect herself until he left and she could re-establish her threshold with energy specifically meant to revoke his invitation.

Iris nearly jumped when the creep knocked on her door.

She smoothed down her dress, wiping her damp palms against the sleek fabric. The dress wasn't as sexy as the spaghetti strap number she'd worn the night before, but it flattered her less than ample figure. More importantly, it was comfortable.

She half hoped that the creep would be gone when she opened the door, but there he stood. She'd thought he was in his thirties, but now she saw that the dark lighting in the bar had been kind to him.

His round face had more lines than she noticed last night. He could have been forty, even a well-preserved fifty. His eyes were a mutable blue-green, wide-set and fathomless. His hair was dark and styled in the standard professional man's cut, not too short and not too long. The kind of haircut barbers could do in their sleep. He held a single yellow rose.

"Friendship?" Iris said, looking at the rose.

The creep smiled. It had been the smile that turned Iris off the night before. That smile said the creep assumed he knew all your darkest desires, and only he could fulfill them.

"The start of something beautiful." He made no move to hand her the rose. "At least I hope so."

Iris swallowed and forced herself to smile back. "Come in," she said, and she stepped back away from the door.

He stepped over her threshold. She could feel when the magic that protected her home winked out.

He held out the rose to her. She took it, careful to check for thorns. She didn't see any.

"I'm not sure I have anything to put this in," she said. No one ever gave her flowers. "If you'll wait for just a moment, I'll go check."

"Take your time," the creep said. "Our dinner reservation's not for an hour."

An hour? Did he really expect his quid pro quo before dinner?

Iris kept the smile plastered on her face as she took the rose into her tiny kitchen. She rooted around in her cabinets for something that would do for a vase. She settled on a tall glass she usually drank ice tea from in the summer.

"Nice little place you've got here," the creep said from her living room. "Cozy."

"Thanks." Iris hated the idea of this man looking over her things. She hoped Ivy was getting a good look of her own.

"Feel like giving me a tour?" he asked.

A tour?

"Not much to see, really." Iris lifted the glass with the rose. It might look good on the mantle, at least for as long as he was here.

The creep met her in the hallway. "You look nice tonight," he said.

His gaze on her body made Iris feel dirty.

He took the glass with the rose in it and put it down on her kitchen counter. "I'd really like that tour," he said. Starting with the bedroom, no doubt.

He took a step forward, and Iris backed up. His grin said he didn't care that he made her nervous when he got close.

She refused to let him back her all the way into her bedroom. She stopped in front of her closed bedroom door. She didn't know why Ivy was still hiding, but enough was enough.

"I don't know what you were expecting from this evening," she said, "but the view from my bed isn't included."

"Oh, c'mon, honey," he said. "A pretty little thing like you, playing dress up just to attract someone like me? You know exactly what I expect."

Playing dress up? "This was a really bad—"

Iris never got to finish the sentence. The smile fell from his face like it had never been there, replaced by an expression that chilled Iris to the bone.

The man was a predator, but more than that, he had a touch of magic. Maybe more than a touch. Enough that he'd not only been able to mask his power, but he'd known she was searching for him. Did he know about Ivy? Had he sensed that Iris had hidden her dead twin's spirit in her carryall the night before?

Had he done something to Ivy now to keep her quiet and helpless? Or worse—had he banished Ivy's spirit liked he'd murdered her body?

He backed Iris up against the wall in her hallway and held her there without touching her with his body. "Now why don't you tell me why you were looking for me?" he asked.

He didn't know about Ivy. Iris should have been reassured, but she'd never been more frightened in her life.

"I wasn't—"

Pain washed through her. Not enough to do any damage, but enough to let her know he could really hurt her if he wanted to.

"I watched you," he said. "For nights on end, did you know that? Someone like you, so uncomfortable in your skin, you stood out." Now he did touch her, but only long enough to yank the wig off her head. "Little girl playing dress up, looking for the big bad wolf. Well, here I am, about to eat you up."

Ivy!

Iris didn't know if Ivy could hear her, but she put all the energy she had into the mental cry. She focused it like she focused her magic when she created the threshold and hoped it was enough.

Cold flooded her bones. Cold, wet, and the absolute darkness of the bottom of the bay swept into Iris as her sister climbed into her body along the bond they shared. Ivy's icy rage merged with Iris's own weak magic, infusing it with a strength Iris had never known.

"You!" Iris said in a voice that wasn't fully her own. "You did this to me!"

The creep's eyes widened in shock and surprise. He made a strangled sound, and now he was the one backing away.

Ivy made Iris follow him. The skin on Iris's arms was bloating, turning fish-belly white. She lifted a hand that was dripping sea water and made a grasping motion. The creep started to choke.

Images invaded Iris's mind. Ivy had never told Iris how she'd died. Iris had never asked. Now she experienced everything firsthand as Ivy's memories became her own.

Iris had thought her sister died because she'd gone home with the wrong man, but Ivy hadn't even paid attention to the creep. She'd been out with people from work, only they'd deserted her. Ivy had left the noisy bar to use her cell to call a cab. The creep had followed her and used his magic to disorient her.

Unlike Iris, Ivy had no magic of her own to fight back. The lack of magic was yet another way the twins weren't quite identical. This time, her individuality had cost Ivy her life.

The creep had taken Ivy to his car. When he was done with her, when his spent and sweaty body was sprawled on top of her bruised and bleeding one, his magic had weakened just enough for Ivy to come back to herself. She realized what he'd done to her, and she began to scream. He'd covered her mouth to shut her up, then he'd pinched her nose closed as well.

Iris realized she was breathing in great gulps of air against the memory of the horrible burning need Ivy had suffered at the end. No one deserved to die like that. To be used and killed and thrown in the bay attached by a meat hook and chain to enough cinder blocks to make sure she never floated to the surface.

Lost and forgotten except by the only person she could reach out to for help. For retribution.

Iris's own rage joined with Ivy's. She squeezed her hand tighter, her enhanced magic cutting off the creep's air even though Iris's hand never touched him.

This bastard had killed Ivy. Killed her sister. Killed *her twin.*

Iris felt him try to fight back. Where his magic had been powerful enough to overcome her before, now he had no chance. Iris had always kept herself tightly controlled. She'd never let emotion fuel her magic. She had no control now. She'd relinquished it to Ivy, and through Iris, Ivy took her revenge.

The creep died horribly. His face turned purple, then the same fish-belly white as Iris's arm. His skin seeped foul-smelling sea water. Huge sores opened on his body as his flesh began to decay. He struggled in their grip, his hands grabbing uselessly at the air until finally his fingers hooked into claws he turned on himself. He raked great gobs of flesh from his neck as he tried to get air into his lungs, but it was far too late. It had been too late before he ever set foot in the apartment.

When he was dead, his eyes milky white and vacant, Iris released her grip. The creep fell to the floor in a boneless heap.

"Big bad wolf," Iris said, and the voice was hers this time, not Ivy's. "You forgot one thing." She stared down at the dead man. "The wolf dies."

Iris collapsed on her sofa, her energy spent. Across the small living room, Ivy began to manifest. Iris understood it would be the last time she'd see her twin.

This Ivy wasn't the bloated, dead thing that had first appeared in the middle of the night. This time the ghost of Iris's dead sister appeared as she had been in life, back when they'd been teenagers. It had been the happiest time of Iris's life. Maybe it had been the happiest time of Ivy's, too.

"Thank you," Ivy said. "I could always count on you, you know. Even more than mom and dad."

The ghost was sitting in the overstuffed chair, her hands folded on her knees. She wasn't smiling but somehow she looked content.

"You're going away," Iris said.

Ivy cocked her head a little to one side. "Yes. At least, I think so. I've never done this before."

"I'm going to miss you," Iris said, realizing it was true. Earlier today, her apartment had seemed too small for the both of them. Now it seemed huge and empty.

"You'll see me again."

Iris tried to smile. She couldn't. "I thought you didn't have a handbook." Difficult to know the rules without a guide. Iris always followed the rules.

Except, of course, when she committed murder.

Ivy started to fade. Iris felt her eyes prick with tears. She wanted to say goodbye, but her voice didn't want to work.

"You need to lighten up, sister," Ivy said. The last little bit of her manifestation faded. Only her voice remained. "Life is too short. Have some fun."

Then Iris's twin was gone.

She wrapped her arms around herself. She'd killed a man. She couldn't let herself lighten up. She'd have to clean things up, and not just the creep's physical remains. The threshold of her home had been damaged in the worst way possible. Iris had allowed it to be breached, and then through the use of the dark emotional energy from Ivy, Iris had taken a life with magic. Thresholds kept things out, but they also kept things in. If Iris didn't cleanse the evil from the apartment, she'd be living with something far worse than her sister's ghost.

Iris tried to get up, but a wave of weariness like she'd never felt before shoved her back down. She had no magic left. She had no energy. She was tired at a cellular level, and no matter how much she wanted to get to work, she'd have to rest before she cleaned up the mess the creep had brought to her home.

She closed her eyes. She just needed a short nap. She still had time. The body wasn't going anywhere.

Iris woke up in the middle of the night. A small flame danced behind the glass in the gas fireplace.

She didn't remember turning the fireplace on. She didn't remember putting on her pajamas before she curled up on the sofa, either.

She started to rub a hand across her face, stopped when she realized her skin was no longer the dead fish white it had been before. She checked both arms. They looked normal.

No five-inch spike-heeled shoes rested by the sofa where she'd kicked them off the night before. The night before, when she'd finally found a man that matched Ivy's vague memories of the man who'd killed her.

The creep Iris had killed earlier.

The creep whose body...

Was no longer in her apartment.

Iris sat bolt upright on the sofa, staring wide-eyed at the place where the creep had fallen to the floor. There wasn't so much as a water stain on her carpet to show where he'd died.

She touched her face. She wasn't wearing any makeup. She remembered putting on at least some for her "date."

Had she dreamed the whole thing? Up to and in-cluding the visits from her ghostly sister?

Iris got to her feet. Her legs felt wobbly and she was ridiculously thirsty. She needed to splash her face with water, and then drink about a gallon of it. Then she could sit down and seriously consider whether she was losing her mind.

The clock on her microwave read a little after two. The kitchen was dark. Iris switched on the overhead light.

There, on her kitchen counter where she remem-bered the creep had left it, a single yellow rose sat in her ice tea glass.

It had all really happened.

Iris didn't know how, but Ivy had taken care of the creep's body. Whether Iris had changed clothes in her sleep or Ivy had somehow managed that trick as well, Iris decided it didn't matter. For a change, her twin had been looking out for someone other than herself.

Iris took the rose from the kitchen and placed it on the mantle. "For Ivy," she said.

The apartment felt too big.

She sat on the sofa and leaned her head back, and thought about whether she should buy herself a pair of shoes with five-inch heels.

DON'T TOUCH

You lift the curtain with the tip of one finger and peer out at the customers ringing the edge of the bar. That's all you can see through the glare of the stage lights.

Emma's up now, dancing around the pole like it could rub her back and pay her mortgage and put her kids through school, and maybe it can because no man's ever gonna do those things for her, like no one's ever gonna do them for you, but it's all you got, and you take what you can get.

The customers look the same as last night's and the night before. Middle-age losers, their mouths slack, hands cupped around their drinks, staring up at

Emma with so much naked want in their faces, it makes you sick.

Cigarette smoke curls around Emma's ankles like so many fingers pulling at her. That'll be you out there in five minutes once Emma's done with her routine and she goes out on the floor so the men beyond the bar can stuff dollar bills under the elastic of her G-string and pretend that fleeting touch is enough.

How many of them would want to touch her if they knew she went home with you?

Would it matter, or would they pay more to watch?

Seeing Emma on stage shouldn't get you hot and bothered, but it does. You run your tongue over your dry lips, and your breasts swell without conscious thought.

You can make yourself into anything, anyone, and right now you want to be the person Emma loves to touch. She knows you as you really are and loves you anyway.

You try to tell yourself that's good enough, but

sometimes you make yourself into a man just so Emma can remember what it's like to have a man inside her who loves her, not one who uses her for a punching bag.

You don't stay a man long, though, because to you, men are the things that stare up at you while you dance and whirl on that pole, who'd pay extra to put their hands on the parts of you that belong to Emma alone.

Emma's music finishes and so does she, stretched out on her belly on the bar, her ass in the air, and you don't have to see the predatory gleam in her eyes as she looks out over her audience to know that it's there. Emma likes turning men on, tells you she feeds off the electricity of all that pent-up want. You love her, so you believe her, even though you're jealous of every man who's ever seen that look on her face and thought it was meant for him.

The spotlights swing off Emma and toward the crack in the curtains where you wait. You stay safe behind the heavy black fabric until you hear the opening bars of your music. You take a deep breath, paste on the sultry smile that's become your trade-mark, and stride on stage like you own it.

The energy you've stored watching Emma dance invigorates your step, accentuates the sway of your hips, and you toss your hair that was blonde this morning but now shines raven black under the harsh stage lights.

Emma slides against you as she makes her way off stage, and you swear you feel an electric current at her touch. You want to turn around and follow her, take her all the way back to the dressing room and do things to each other that the men in the audience can't even imagine, but you stay on stage.

You need this job. The owner's a good sort, he watches out for his girls which can't be said of most club owners in The Shadows, so you bump and grind and hold your shape for the entire dance even though the more the customers remove what little clothes you're wearing with their eyes, the more you want to shift your skin to create a hard, impenetrable shell so that no one can touch you or see you or hurt you.

No one but Emma.

The music's more upbeat than you'd like. It's hard to dance sexy to the old rock 'n roll tunes the owner prefers, but Emma manages it, so you do too. You're more flexible than Emma with her human body, and you use the pole like you were born to do nothing else, and maybe you weren't.

When the dance is over, you glide down the steps at the back of the bar. Emma's already out in the audience, taking drink orders from the tables in the back, lining up the kind of dances that happen in thc room off the side of the stage where the dancers do little more than dry hump some poor guy with more money than brains, always telling them no touching, no touching, no touching.

You want to be anywhere but on the floor, but the owner's at his table in the back corner watching, making sure the customers stay in line and the girls do their job.

He's the biggest dwarf you've ever seen, some say he isn't a dwarf at all but something far more dangerous. All you know is you don't want to make him mad and make him fire you because then you won't see Emma again, you know that, so you find a table and smile and flirt and entice stupid men to spend their money on you.

The good ones want to buy you drinks, and you let them. The drinks are watered down. You could drink your weight each night and never get a buzz, but your people don't get drunk easy anyway, and the more drinks sold, the better the owner likes it. The more he'll keep you on even though he hates changelings, though he's never told you that to your face, something to do with when he was a cop even though he isn't anymore.

You don't bother to tell him that not all changelings are bad.

Sometimes the bad people are just people.

You spot one at a table in the back looking at you with hungry eyes. You recognize something in him that speaks to you in ways you don't understand, and that makes you nervous.

You give him a quick grin and start to turn away, but he beckons to you with a crooked finger, probably thinks he's cute, so you put a little more sway into your hips as you walk his way. You grow your grin into a smile that hurts your face but you keep it in place, and you ask him what his pleasure is just like you do with every customer.

You put a little more sex into your smile when he says, "You."

You tell him the price, and he pulls twenties out of his wallet and slides them beneath the elastic of your G-string.

His thick fingers are cold and rough, not fisherman rough, you've had experience with that, every dancer's had experience with that, the club's so close to the docks that some nights all the men at the tables have rough hands and smell of dead fish and musty sea water. You take this man's thick-fingered hand and lead him to the back room, feeling the dwarf's eyes on you from his corner table, always watching to make sure no one hurts his girls, and how can you tell him that just working here hurts?

You try not to notice details about your cus-tomer, but you can't help it. His eyes are dark, deep blue or black, you can't tell in the low lighting of the club's back room, and his hair is close-cropped and spikey with so much product that when you put your hands on the sides of his face, his hair pokes your fingers. He hasn't shaved in a few days, and beneath the growing stubble, his skin is rough and leathery.

You move your hands to his shoulders, lean forward so that your breasts are right in his face, and whisper in his ear that he can't touch, don't touch, never touch, then you start your dry-humping dance over the lap of his trousers.

You've never understood men who crave this kind of not-touching, and you wonder what in this man's past would make him settle for being so close to something he obviously wants so badly but isn't allowed to have.

You notice that he has his eyes closed and is breathing hard through his nose, his nostrils flared, and for the first time you notice that his nose is crooked, like it's been broken more than once. You wonder how he broke it while you notice other scars on his face, lines that blend in with the creases and folds time has given him, and you wonder what it would be like to have a flawed face you couldn't flow into another shape on a whim.

In the middle of your dance, when you're just getting going good, he asks you if you can be someone else for him, that he'll pay you good. He's still not looking at your face, still has his eyes closed, still breathing through his nose, and you realize he's breathing *you*, smelling the sweat and cheap perfume and alcohol and cigarette smoke that permeates your skin so deep that no amount of scrubbing in a hot shower gets rid of the stench.

Something about the way he says it, the sheer need in his voice, sends a shiver up your spine.

You don't care that he knows you aren't human, this is The Shadows, after all. Most things out after dark on the streets by the docks aren't strictly human, even though you're sure he is, but something about him creeps you out more than just a needy, clutching customer would. You realize he's dangerous, even though he's done nothing to you except fork over cash he doesn't look like he can spare given the threadbare collar of his shirt and his scuffed shoes, and you wonder if he collects weird fucks like other people collect marbles.

You grind down closer on his lap, feeling his need, but you tell him that the boss doesn't like his girls to do more than this, so you can't be his private fantasy.

His eyes fly open. You expect to see anger in them, and yes, there it is, the barely-bottled rage of a frustrated man who can't have everything he wants, but there's something else in there too, a sadness so profound that your own blood runs cold and you want nothing more than to run to Emma and have her enfold you in her strong arms to keep away the bone-chilling emptiness in this man's heart.

He violates the club's rule by grabbing your hips hard enough to leave bruises, if you'd been human, and he pushes you away from him. He gets up, seeming not to care that his lust for you is evident for everyone to see, and he walks straight from the back room through the club and out the front door.

You watch him leave, shaking so hard you think

you might fly apart.

You don't know why, but you feel like you've escaped something you didn't even know was stalking you, and you blow out a deep breath and try to calm your nerves.

You want to take a break in the room in the back.

You want to pack it in for the night, but you haven't earned enough yet and you can't put it all on Emma's back to support the both of you and her kids, too, so you straighten your back and try to make your way into the club like nothing happened even though your guts tells you it did.

The dwarf is watching you intently now, his dark eyes half-hidden in the fleshy folds of his face and the abundance of hair and beard that billow out around his head, but all you feel from him is concern. You know he'd toss anyone out who ever laid a hand on you. You don't tell him what the customer did, or how it makes you feel, you just smile at the dwarf and pick up where you left off, making rounds of the tables and separating men from their money.

The customer never quite leaves your thoughts.

After your last pole dance of the evening, Emma's waiting for you behind the heavy black curtains. She pulls you into an embrace, holds you close and kisses you, and you almost, almost, *almost* forget the customer while you're kissing.

You're both done for the night, so you dress and chatter and laugh while the dwarf kicks the last of the straggling customers out and locks up the front. You and Emma leave by the side exit to the alley between the club and the magic supply shop next door where the wizard wannabes buy supplies they'll never know how to use.

Emma's happy, she made a lot in tips, and she wants to take a cab home. She says she'll blow you in the back seat, and you can see how her dark eyes shine with pent-up sexual energy. Emma's done more backroom dances than you have, and they always turn her on.

You consider her offer right up until you see the lone cab waiting by the curb in front of the club.

You have better eyesight than humans, you don't know why, but you can see the face of the cabbie sitting in his darkened cab, and you recognize the customer who put his hands on you. You tell Emma that you want to walk, that it will be fun, and you'll make it up to her later. You know in that moment that you'd promise her anything to keep her out of that cab.

Emma looks at you like you've lost your mind. She knows how tired you get after a night on your feet, and you've never turned down a blow job from her before.

You can't tell her your fears about the cabbie because Emma's not afraid of any man, and she'd take the cab just to show you there's nothing to be afraid of, but you know there is.

You know because in another life, before you met Emma and learned you could care about some- one else more than life itself, you were the thing to be afraid of. The thing that reshaped herself into the lives she took without a second thought, only now you can't imagine life without Emma in it, and that's made you weak.

You tell Emma that you want a bite to eat before

you head home, that you're famished even though you know you won't be able to keep a bite of it down, and she relents.

You have a favorite diner a block away, a hole in the wall place that won't let the junkies in even after midnight. Where the coffee's good and the working girls mingle with the strippers, and no one's pimp beats anyone because the cops who camp out in the back booth only look the other way if no one's getting hurt.

Only tonight none of the cops are in their booth and the working girls look nervous. You and Emma sit at the end of the counter, and while Emma orders for the both of you, you listen to the conversations ebbing and flowing around you.

You learn that the body of a high-class working girl was pulled from the dark waters of Moretown Bay. A changeling, like you. Strangled. One of the few ways someone whose flesh can flow around a wound can be killed.

You shiver. Emma asks what's wrong. Even though the night air off the bay is cold, it's warm in the diner.

You don't tell her you think the cabbie had something to do with the dead working girl. You know you can't prove it, it's just a feeling, the recognition by one former predator of another currently on the prowl, but you've never been so glad in your life that you didn't take the cab.

You tell Emma that a goose must have walked over your grave, and she laughs, calls you a silly goose yourself, and plants a kiss on the side of your facc.

You consider whether the cabbie will come back, whether it's time to find a new job, but as you eat a tuna sandwich you don't really want, you understand that he won't.

Just for a moment, back when he asked you to be someone else, he made himself vulnerable, let you see inside his pain. He won't want that to happen again. For now, you're safe. You and Emma.

When you're in bed next to her, after you've satisfied her need for a man this night and she's sleeping, you change back to the female form you've come to think of as your true self. You briefly consider setting a trap for the cabbie and taking care of him, you used to do that as easily as you now work the pole, but you're no longer that brave. Something about the cabbie frightens you at a gut level, and you've become a coward.

Stretched out in the near dawn beside your lover, you finally realize a fundamental truth.

While you can change yourself to look like anyone else, while you used to mimic people so perfectly that you took over their very existence, the one thing you cannot change is the person you are inside. Emma loves the person you are, and because of her love, you care too much about Emma and the kids sleeping in the next room, two perfect, miniature versions of their mom. You can't risk their lives.

You tell yourself it doesn't matter, that it's up to the cops to catch the cabbie before he kills again, because you know he will kill again, you saw it in his face.

You tell yourself it's none of your business, but

you know better.

You call yourself a coward and a liar, and you know that's not who Emma loves.

You dress quietly so not to wake her. You look in on the children once before you leave. You'd like to give notice at the club, but you don't want the dwarf to talk you out of it.

You take on a different appearance and start walking the streets at night. You keep your eyes open for the cabbie, but you can't spot him. You turn tricks to earn enough money to keep yourself in the crummy little hotel room that reeks of the fish market three floors below. You miss Emma with an ache that's overpowering most nights when you finally go to bed alone. You can't go near the club, even in your transformed state, because you can't chance seeing her alone, or worse, seeing her with someone new.

Finally, one night, you spot a cab parked down by a commercial pier where sailboats and power-boats are docked. You linger in the dark beneath a burned-out street lamp. Your eyes pick out the shape of a rowboat pulling through the black water of the Bay. The cabbie's little more than a solid back silhouette against the blacker night, but you recognize him.

You change your shape into something you think he'll like. You lean against his cab, the metal cold against your bare thighs, the dress almost too short to cover your ass.

He's surprised to see you. You tell him your last john dumped you on the docks and stiffed you, not in a good way, can you give a girl a lift? The cabbie doesn't smile, doesn't open the door of his cab.

"Don't you think I've learned how to spot you?" he asks. "No matter what shape you take? Don't you think I know who you are?"

You don't have a weapon, but that never stopped you before. You can change your hands into sharp blades, and you start to do that but the cabbie's on you, he's fast, oh so fast, and *strong*. His hands are around your throat, choking, squeezing, and for the first time you realize not only how thick his fingers are but how big his knuckles are too, and you understand that he must have been a boxer, a fighter, and you wonder if anyone ever knocked him out.

You see a rage in his face that wasn't there before, not even when you stopped him from touching you in the club.

"Why couldn't you just leave me alone?" he yells at you, spittle flying from his lips. "Why can't you all just leave me alone?"

You want to tell him that you've made a mistake, that all you want to do is go home to Emma and her children and beg their forgiveness, forget that you ever met the cabbie, ever made him angry, but you can't say anything. Your thoughts are getting fuzzy, the night darker than it should be, and you've forgotten something important. Something you meant to do. Something you meant to shift into.

When you remember, you barely have the strength to bring your fingers together, to concentrate enough to make your flesh flow, to flatten the bones of your hand and fuse them together, to lengthen and thicken the nails on your fingers.

When you stab your hand into the cabbie's belly,

you're not sure if your new bladed arm is formed enough to do much damage.

The cabbie grunts and jerks, folding in on himself, and you feel warmth surround your sharp hand as the cabbie's blood flows down your arm. His terrible grip on your throat lessens, and you cough. Human or changeling, everything needs to breathe, and you gasp huge lungfuls of cold night air.

The cabbie curses you, and blood dribbles from his mouth as he talks. He tries to stumble away, and your bladed arm comes loose from his belly with a horrible squelching sound.

You never killed like this before. You were neat and clean, and you took lives swiftly so that your victims didn't suffer. The cabbie will suffer, and for the first time in your life, you're glad.

Down here on the docks, no one cares enough to pay attention. If anyone saw what you did, they won't call the cops. No sirens or flashing lights will interrupt the cabbie's slow death, not in The Shadows. He collapses on the rough boards of the pier, and his blood continues to flow.

Once you're sure he's unconscious, you shove his body off the edge of the dock, and you wait until you hear it splash in the black water below. You know you should have waited until he was dead, but you're appalled by what you've done. You hunted the cabbie and killed him, not to steal his identity but to prevent him from killing, a distinction that will not make one bit of difference if you're caught.

You have to leave.

You shift into another form, a male form. You steal clothes from a homeless man sleeping off a bender, and you walk to the bus station. You pass by the club but you don't linger. This is as close as you will get to saying goodbye.

You have just enough money to buy a ticket that will take you into the next state where you'll stop at the next city big enough for you to blend in and start a new life. You try to forget about Emma as the bus takes you out of the city, but your heart is breaking. You're still a coward. You're still running away.

You tell yourself it doesn't matter. You've lost the only person you've ever loved, you lost the life you thought you'd made for yourself, but none of that matters.

The only thing that matters is that Emma and her children are safe, that's enough for you, and you tell yourself that over and over again as the miles between you and Emma roll out behind the bus.

One day you hope you'll believe it.

Ties That Bind

The first hint of trouble came from Gris in Research and Development.

"We're having a bit of a problem getting the enchantments to stick to the new cuffs," he said to me in an early morning phone call.

I've never done mornings well, but when you're the wizard in charge of the largest magical enhancements company in Moretown Bay, and a woman in a man's profession to boot, whether you do mornings well or not doesn't matter one damn bit.

I leaned back in my leather chair and gazed out my tenth floor office window at the overcast sky. The streets below were still wet from last night's rain. I could almost smell the wet asphalt. It would probably rain again today. I pinched the bridge of my nose against an impending headache that wasn't all sinuses.

"Is it the alloy or the spell?" I asked Gris.

"Can't tell yet," he said. "We're still testing. Just thought you should know, Nell. Considering."

Yeah. Considering.

My company had a contract with the city to supply enhanced weapons and restraints to the police department. Research and Development had been testing redesigned handcuffs. Lighter weight with an easy snap-close lock, the new handcuffs were supposed to address problems the cops had with the old handcuff design.

Personally, I thought any set of handcuffs that could keep a changeling in its true shape or prevent a wizard from casting a spell to escape custody were good enough, but my father built this company by supplying our customers with whatever they wanted. And what the customer I had a meeting with later today wanted was new and better handcuffs.

"Keep me informed," I said, and I hung up the phone.

I unlocked the bottom drawer in my desk and took out the thick, three-ring binder I kept there under lock and key.

To the uninitiated, the binder looked like nothing more than what a high school student might carry around in a backpack. But instead of notes on Shakespeare, calculus, and the culture of ancient Rome, this notebook was chock full of page after page of spells and instructions written in a tiny, crabbed hand, all neatly separated into categories by brightly-colored index tabs. My father had been anal in the extreme. This was his spell book. What he'd built this company with.

And what he'd handed over to his only daughter when he died.

I glanced at my watch. Eight-fifteen. I had a little less than two hours before my meeting with the city's purchasing director. If the problem was in the enchantment, the answer should be in the spell book. I might not be powerful enough to cast the spell myself, but that didn't mean I couldn't spot a problem with the enchantment.

I opened the binder and started to read.

Templeton Rae showed up for our meeting ten minutes early. Not surprising. Templeton was a born pencil pusher. He probably dreamed about numbers in neat, orderly columns that always balanced and never dipped over into the red. Tall and gaunt looking with a movie villain mustache, Templeton handled the city's multi-million dollar purchasing contracts like every penny the city spent came from his own pocket.

I met him in the ninth floor conference room. Outside of my office, this corner conference room had the best view in the building. If the sky hadn't started pouring rain an hour ago, we could have seen the snow-tipped peaks of the mountain range to the east from one set of floor to ceiling windows and across the bay to the exclusive homes on Marlette Island out the other. The view today wasn't quite as impressive. Still, it never hurt to treat Templeton Rae to the best.

He didn't shake my hand when I came into the conference room, not a good sign. Still, I smiled my warmest smile and asked him about his family.

"Fine, they're all fine, but let's get to the point," he said as we sat down—on opposite sides of the conference table. "I've received a bid for light-weight, enchanted handcuffs that's quite a bit lower than yours."

I tried to keep my face impassive even though my heart rate went through the roof. Our contracts with the city for the various enhanced items we produce comprised more than half of my company's annual revenue. If we lost the handcuff contract, that would just be the start of a long, slow slide into downsizing and maybe even bankruptcy.

"I didn't know you put the job out to bid," I said.

"We put every job out to bid."

"After you sign the contract?"

Templeton had the good graces to look uncomfortable.

"This bid did come in quite late. I wouldn't have looked at it if the numbers weren't significantly lower."

"How much lower?"

"Significantly."

I only had so much I could cut off my bottom line, and Templeton knew it. He was fishing, trying to see how low I would go.

"We've got a signed contract," I said. "It's a little late to renegotiate this deal, don't you think?"

Templeton did what I like to think of as a mental shrug. He leaned back in his chair just the slightest and the tension in his face loosened a fraction. If he'd been a less-seasoned negotiator, he might have actually twitched his shoulders, but he didn't.

"It's never too late to renegotiate, you know that, Nell," he said. "Besides... the delivery date's in a week, and your people haven't spoken to anyone in Receiving about when to expect shipment. That's not like you. It makes people on my end nervous."

It made *him* nervous, we both knew that. What I didn't know was that no one had been in touch with the city about the shipment, and that made me nervous.

Templeton was right. This wasn't how my company operated. I wondered exactly how long Gris had known about the problem with the enchantments, and why he had waited until this morning to tell me. What exactly was he hiding? If we couldn't deliver the cuffs on time, that gave the city a reason to back out of the deal.

This was all too coincidental. Never trust a coincidence, my father used to say. And Templeton showing up the same morning Gris told me he had a problem with the cuffs was a damn big coincidence.

Whether I wanted to believe it or not, the conclusion was inevitable.

I had a spy.

Gris Mellion was my father's oldest friend. They'd gone to school together, raised hell—almost literally—together, and been inseparable until graduation when they went their separate ways, my father to start a family and this business, Gris to travel the world and continue learning how to be the best wizard he could be.

Unfortunately for Gris, the best wizard he could be wasn't all that great. Sure, he could learn incantations and he had great ideas. He just couldn't put his ideas to practical use. My father could.

When Gris came back from his travels with a dozen sketch books filled with vague ideas, a leatherbound spell book less than half the size of my father's binder, and no money in his pocket, my father gave Gris a job as head of Research and Development.

Together again, the two of them clicked. With Gris's ideas and my father's practical know how, they invented most of the magical weapons the police department used every day.

After my father died, I inherited his share of the patents for those weapons and the income generated from licenses for their use. I kept Gris on, made sure he had assistants with the same practical know how my father had, and I wrote a hefty bonus structure into his employment contract commensurate with the income his inventions brought the company. Gris had as much riding on this contract with the city as I did.

After my meeting with Templeton Rae, I rode the elevator down to the sixth floor lab that Research and Development called home. I found Gris swearing at the top of his lungs at a vaguely handcuff-shaped wad of green goo.

Gris barely looked up when I stopped on the other side of the pristine white workbench in his office.

"Let me guess," I said, nodding at the green goo. "That's the alloy that won't behave?"

Gris looked every bit like a fairytale wizard. Long white beard, long white hair, gnarled knuckles, wire-rimmed spectacles perched on the end of a prominent nose. Gris wasn't really all that old, not for a wizard, but according to my mother, the things Gris and my father did in their young and stupid days took a toll on both of them.

Although my mother never said, I got the feeling

the things that made Gris look old before his time were the same things that took my father's life.

"Damn stuff," Gris said.

He waved his hand over the goo, muttered an incantation, and with a whiff of ozone the stuff blinked out of existence.

"Back to Mineralogy," Gris said in response to my stare.

I had a strict rule—the company recycled whenever possible. Gris hadn't really zapped the goo off the face of the earth, although he probably wanted to. Instead he'd reduced the stuff to its component minerals to be used in something a little more practical. Like a paperclip.

"Figure out what's wrong yet?" I asked.

Gris wiped his mouth with the back of his hand. "I'm using the same enchantment we've been using on handcuffs since the day we invented the things. The enchantment works." He pointed to a length of silver chain, the links barely larger than the ones in the necklace I wore. "Try wrapping that around your wrists," he said.

I held my wrists together and Gris looped the chain around them. As soon as the chain wrapped around once, it started to emanate a faint green glow. The binding enchantment was working. I shouldn't be able to use any magic as long as the chain was wrapped around me.

I tried a simple incantation to transport a cup of tea from my office to the table in front of me. Nothing. I tried moving my wrists, but the chain held tight. I tried breaking the chain, it was flimsy enough. No go. The chain might as well have been made of titanium.

"So it's not the enchantment," I said as Gris unwrapped the chain and the enchantment went dormant. I had a thin cut on the back of my right hand where I had tried to get free. It stung like a paper cut. I rubbed at it to make the sting go away.

"And it's not the cuffs," Gris said.

He reached into a cardboard box on the table behind him and took out a pair of the redesigned handcuffs. The cuffs were noticeably thinner than the last generation we produced for the city. They felt just as sturdy when Gris snapped one cuff around my left wrist. Unfortunately, it took only a minor incantation on my part to unlock the cuff. It wouldn't keep any magic user restrained for more than half a heartbeat.

"But we put the two together...."

Gris held his hand over the cuffs and murmured the spell for the enchantment. The handcuffs took on a green glow for a moment like they were supposed to, and then the cuffs seemed to absorb the glow—again, like they were supposed to. But as the last of the glow faded, the metal handcuffs seemed to shiver, and the cuffs simply melted. Another mess of green goo.

Great. Just great. "And you didn't tell me about this earlier because..."

Gris shot a long-suffering look over my shoulder. I turned around to see a stack of cardboard boxes a good six feet high against the side wall of Gris's office. The sides of the boxes bowed out, damp and disgusting looking, and now that I was turned in their direction, I could smell the same whiff of ozone I'd smelled when Gris made the goo disappear.

"We didn't have this problem until yesterday," Gris said. "I enchanted these cuffs last week, Shipping packed them up, had them inventoried and invoiced, ready to go. I got a call yesterday afternoon from Eleanor wanting to know who the practical joker was so she could roast his head on a spit."

Eleanor, the manager in Shipping, was a dwarf with a head for details and a quick temper. Nobody, including me, liked a call from a pissed-off Eleanor.

"And the cuffs were fine last week," I said.

Gris nodded. "We over-produced on the cuffs, so I tried the enchantments again last night and this morning. This time..." He sighed. "Well, you saw what happened. The Production Department's working overtime recreating the cuffs, but without the enchantment, we might as well melt them down into key chains for all the good they'll do."

"Who knows the enchantment besides you?"

"No one," Gris said.

"You have it written down anywhere?"

"No." He sounded upset that I asked.

The magic-inhibiting enchantment was my company's biggest trade secret. My father had stumbled on the spell while he was playing around with another spell—one that was supposed to inhibit the growth of weeds, of all things. The enchantment worked by interrupting a magic user's connection with the natural world. As long as whatever held the enchantment was latched in a complete circle around a magic user—like handcuffs, or the chain Gris had wrapped around my wrist—the spell was complete and the magic user's connection to the source of their magic was interrupted.

The spell was written down in my father's binder. Gris had memorized the spell after my father died so that he could perform the incantations. Gris was the only person I trusted with the spell, and he'd promised me he would never tell another living soul.

If someone knew the spell, not only could they use it to make their own enchanted weapons—like the bidder Templeton Rae told me about—but they could, in theory, add an enchanted mineral to the alloy for the cuffs that would render the spell inert.

"And I suppose you've checked the formula for the alloy, made sure nothing's in the mix that would cause the green goop effect. "

Gris shook his head. "I've gone over it, Mineralogy's gone over it. There's nothing in the cuffs that should be causing this."

Nothing should, but something was. If it wasn't Gris and it wasn't something in the cuffs, that meant I had a magic user, and a pretty powerful one at that, interfering with the incantation at a level far beyond what I could detect.

I needed help.

It was time to talk to my father.

Fortune tellers were a dime a dozen in the city. Some were legitimate, most were bogus. My mother was the real thing.

When I was little, my mother would annoy me no end by grounding me for things I hadn't done yet. Oh, I'd thought about doing them, even worked out schemes in my mind for ways I could trick my parents, but it wasn't until I was nine years old that I realized my mother was a precog.

After my father died, I spent a good deal of time being angry with my mother for her apparent lack of grief over her husband's death. She only laughed at me and told me the world was a far bigger place than I could see. One night she brought a crystal ball to my house, made me sit with her at my dining room table, and showed me what she meant.

I canceled my afternoon appointments, made sure my father's spell book was locked up nice and tight, with a second level of security spells just in case, and took the ferry to my mother's house on Marlette Island.

"I need to talk to dad," I said when she answered the door.

She raised an eyebrow, but I must have looked harried enough she didn't grill me. She took my soggy raincoat, made me a cup of tea—decaf—and led me into what she called her parlor.

The room was circular, lined with floor to ceiling

bookshelves loaded with decades' worth of books—fiction; no spell books for my mother—and French doors that overlooked her gardens. The gardener, a wood elf with long, flowing, brunette hair, was at work in the rain planting spring seedlings.

The scene looked peaceful. Sometimes I wished I could be like that—impervious to the weather and the bottom line, just living in touch with nature. Unfortunately, my abilities were more in tune with the business world.

My mother sat in a deeply-padded wingback chair. Her crystal ball rested on a small round table next to her. I sat in another wingback chair, this one not as well-used or as well-padded, the hot cup of tea cradled in my hands.

"I don't suppose you want to tell me what this is all about," my mother said.

"We're having a problem with one of dad's spells," I said. I didn't want to tell her all of my suspicions. While I knew my mother was the real deal, I didn't want to influence her in any way. When she contacted my father, I wanted to know I was really talking to him.

My mother sat back in her chair and closed her eyes. She didn't need to touch the crystal ball, unlike the charlatans who hovered over their tables and wailed and fluttered their fingers over crystal that remained stubbornly clear. No, my mother just closed her eyes and concentrated. I suppose it helped that my father had been—and still was—the one true love of her life. It gave her a connection to him that no one else had. Even me.

I sat still and quiet, held my tea but didn't drink any of it. I watched the gardener walk on top of the muddy ground, his boots clean, no footprints in his wake. He seemed to commune with each seedling he put in the ground. It could have been my imagination, but I almost sensed the conversations they were having.

The air in the parlor suddenly seemed heavy and the light had an odd quality, like someone had layered more clouds in between the earth and the sun. My heart started beating faster. I had an odd taste in my mouth, something metallic and unpleasant. In the garden the wood elf stopped in the middle of putting a seedling in the ground, his head tilted like he was listening to something only he could hear.

I glanced at the crystal ball and gasped. The inside was roiling with dark clouds shot through with bolts of lightning.

That had never happened before.

A loud, ugly laugh echoed in the room. My mother's head lolled sideways, her mouth open and slack.

"Oh, Nelly, Nelly, who have you come looking for?"

The voice coming out of my mother's mouth was just as ugly as the laugh. It made my skin crawl.

"Who are you?" I asked.

"Don't you recognize your dear old dad?"

This was not my father.

"Who are you?" I asked again.

I felt power crackle around the room. I started to say an incantation to create a layer of protection around my mother.

"I wouldn't do that if I were you."

I watched as my mother's face took on a blue tinge, and I realized she wasn't breathing.

"Stop that!" I shouted.

I must have dropped my tea cup. I dimly heard it shatter on the hardwood floor. It was enough to break my concentration, and the spell I had started to cast drifted away from me.

Color returned to my mother's cheeks.

"You've been a bad, bad girl, playing with things beyond your comprehension. I've put a stop to that."

What?

"Who *are* you?"

The air coalesced in front of me. Mist formed into shape, and shape took on substance.

My father's face. The thing in the room with us wore my father's face.

The French doors burst open, and the wood elf practically flew into the room on a gust of wind and rain. He shouted something in a language I didn't understand and threw a handful of greenery at the misty shape of my father's face.

The mist exploded in a barrage of light and sound.

I screamed and clamped my hands over my ears, shut my eyes, but I could still see my father's face.

Only it wasn't his face as I remembered it. This face was evil and hateful, the eyes full of vengeful fury, the mouth filled with sharpened teeth. It was the stuff of nightmares.

When I opened my eyes the presence was gone. The wood elf crouched on the floor with my mother cradled in his arms.

I crawled over to her, touched her face. Her skin was cold and clammy, her breaths shallow, but at least she was breathing.

"Mom?"

It took a minute before her eyelids fluttered open. I watched as realization hit her, and she began to cry.

In an odd reversal of parenting roles, I fixed my mother a strong cup of tea. The wood elf, who introduced himself as Diray Gant, brought a blanket to wrap around my mother's shoulders as she sat huddled at the kitchen table, then he brought in a potted geranium from the garden to put on the table next to her. She tried to smile at him, but her eyes were too haunted for the smile to work. He sat down next to her and held her hand, and I realized he was probably more than just her gardener.

"What was that?" I asked after I got a cup of tea for myself.

My mother shared a look with Diray. He nodded almost imperceptibly.

"I need to tell you something about your father. Your father and Gris, actually," she said. "You've known all your life that your father dabbled in things he probably shouldn't have."

My father's "wild days" were legendary. But apparently not everything had made it into legend.

"There's a dark side to the magical world," my mother said. "I don't have to tell you that. You work with the police and the police deal with it every day. The criminals they arrest, the ones they use your cuffs to restrain—that's just the tip of that side of the magical realm. Your father was a curious man. Both of them were. He and Gris. So sure of themselves. Young and cocky, they thought they could just go on a little vacation and none of what they did would touch them."

She took a sip of tea. I didn't want mine any-more. A sick little ball of dread had started to squeeze my insides into a tight knot.

"Of course, it did touch them," my mother said. "It took Gris's youth, and eventually it took your fa-ther's life. I believe deep down inside he knew it would, which is why he spent so much time and en-ergy developing things to contain the evil he'd tasted." She looked at me, her eyes moist and sad. "He didn't want it to touch you, to touch us."

It made sense. Most of the patents my father and Gris had registered were for devices that contained magic. The story about how he developed the incan-tation as an accident was just that — a story, no more real that the fiction my mother loved to read. He'd been looking for the right spell all along.

I took a deep breath. "So that was my father?"

My mother shook her head. "No. No, that wasn't your father. It was just using him. Hitching a ride on his memory to frighten you away."

"It?"

"You don't want to know more than that. Trust me on this, Nell."

I saw the fear in my mother's eyes. I believed her.

So whatever it was, it was using my father to get to me. To get to us.

Using him.

To get to all of us? Including Gris?

If it had touched my father, had it touched Gris?

What if Gris had been saying the wrong incantation all along and he didn't even know it?

I put my tea down on the table and got up.

"I have to go." I kissed my mother on her forehead. "Take care of her," I said to Diray.

"I will," he said. His voice was melodious and soothing. He looked at me with his grey eyes. "Take care of yourself as well."

I hoped I'd be able to do that. First I had to save my father's oldest friend, and with any luck, I'd be able to save my company along the way.

By the time I got back to the office, the workday was over. The nine to five employees were gone, but I knew I'd find Gris still hard at work in his lab. First I wanted to stop by my office. There was a section in my father's spell book I needed to read.

When I'd inherited the spell book, it had taken me months to read through all of my father's notes. The last section, separated from the rest by a red tab, contained only a few pages of lined paper. The pages were blank.

I'd asked my mother about it, but she simply said that section was for spells my father hadn't invented yet. On the ferry ride back across the bay, I'd started to wonder if that section wasn't blank after all, only hidden. Before today I had no reason to doubt my mother's explanation.

I knew a spell for revealing hidden text. If that

section held what I thought it did—my father's notes on what he learned of dark magic—I might need them.

I threw my damp raincoat across the back of one of the visitor chairs in front of my desk. I didn't care where the water dripped. I dug my desk keys out of my purse and sat down in my chair before I even realized something was wrong.

My desk drawer had been jimmied open, the security spells shattered.

My father's spell book was missing.

Gris!

I ran to the elevator and punched the button for the sixth floor with a trembling finger. The elevator seemed to barely move, yet before I was ready, the doors opened on the lab.

The stench was overpowering. The smell of ozone from the green goo was magnified a thousand fold. All the lights in the lab were blazing bright. A sound like thunder crackled through overheated air.

I found Gris in his office. My father's spell book lay open to the red-tabbed section on Gris's worktable. Words crawled across the page as Gris stood over the book, hands extended, sweat running down his face. The wispy ends of his hair and beard seemed to float on unseen currents of air.

"Gris!"

He flinched when I called out his name. I realized he'd been muttering something under his breath. He glanced up at me, his eyes wide and wild.

"It's our fault, Nell," he said. "I had a dream this afternoon. A vision. I realized what happened to the spell. Who our 'competitor' was." He laughed, not a sane sound. It sent shivers down my spine. "We've seen him before. Your father and I. I know how to fix it."

Gris had never been the best wizard. Even I knew what he was attempting was beyond his ability.

"Gris, stop. Please stop."

The air grew heavy, and the fluorescent lights dimmed. Lightning began to crackle along the edges of my vision.

"I can beat this," Gris said. "I have to, don't you see? I'm all that stands in its way."

Mist swirled around us and began to coalesce.

I darted forward and grabbed the spell book from Gris. The writing disappeared as soon as I took it from him.

Dammit. I had no time, no time left at all.

I cast the revealing spell as quickly as I could. The air became thick and hard to breathe. I held the spell book in one hand as words reformed on the blank paper. I scanned the pages until I found the incantation I knew had to be there.

"No!" Gris shouted. "It will know you too, don't you see? *It will know you!*"

I looked up in time to see the mist form into the shape that wore my father's face. The horrible thing smiled at me.

"Go back to hell," I said, and I began to cast the spell that would carry out my words.

The thing screamed. All the windows in the sixth floor blew out with the force of its fury.

I felt something wrap slimy tendrils around my neck and squeeze.

Blood pounded in my ears, and the unpleasant

taste of metal filled my mouth, but still I murmured the words of the incantation.

"No! You can't have her!"

My vision was beginning to darken, but I still could see well enough to watch Gris rush the thing out of the corner of my eye.

Then I saw something I will never forget.

I saw my father.

Not the thing wearing my father's face, but my father—ghostly and indistinct, but *there*.

Gris must have seen him too. He reached for my father with one hand and for me with the other. Power surged through me like lightening.

The tendrils around my neck loosened. My throat was raw, my voice nearly gone.

"Finish it, sweetheart," I heard my father say.

I did. The room exploded in light even as I drifted into darkness.

We delivered the redesigned handcuffs to the city two days early. It took Production three days of working around the clock to reproduce the hardware. I didn't sleep for the two days it took me to cast the enchantments on each box of cuffs.

I called Templeton Rae myself to tell him we were fulfilling our contract. Templeton actually seemed relieved.

"I hope you'll give us an opportunity to bid on the next available contract," I said.

My voice was still a little hoarse. If Templeton noticed, he didn't mention it. Maybe he thought I was getting a cold.

"The city always welcomes your bids," he said. "You're known for the quality and integrity of your work."

I wondered again if someone in our company was leaking information to Templeton. At this point I didn't care. Let them leak what happened on the sixth floor. Maybe it would give Templeton second thoughts about dealing with the wrong manufacturer.

I leaned back in my desk chair and stared out at the city, and wondered if it was all worth it.

My father's spell book was back in my bottom

drawer. Gris had survived, but he wouldn't be coming back to work. He had a permanent tremor in his hands, and I saw the fear in his eyes when I visited him in the hospital.

Gris, whose mind had been failing for years, had finally gone up against something too big for him, and he knew it. He'd found his limits. I'd make sure he was taken care of for the rest of his life.

My mother said my father was truly gone now. She seemed diminished somehow, even though she still had Diray and the house and her garden. And me. She still had me, although I was diminished, too.

Gris had been right. The thing I'd banished knew me now. It knew the taste of my magic, just like I knew its taste, too.

That was the final ingredient in the enchantment spell for the cuffs—the taste of the magic it was meant to contain.

My father and Gris had been the only wizards I knew who could cast that particular spell. I'd tried over the years, but I'd never been successful.

Until now.

And now I knew why.

The real containment spell was in the red-tabbed section of my father's spell book. The spell I thought Gris had been using all these years—the one I'd thought I wasn't powerful enough to cast—was a decoy.

I'd been powerful enough to cast the real enchantment all along. I just had to take a walk on the dark side before I could use it. I had truly become my father's daughter.

I turned the key to lock up the spell book. I thought about my father as a young man dabbling in things he couldn't begin to understand. I thought about the criminals who didn't understand any better than my father, but who gave their lives over to dark magic willingly for a little money or power.

Was I any different? I thought about the work my company did, the lives we saved. Was it worth the dark owning a piece of my soul?

Ask me in fifty years or so, but I have a feeling the answer will be yes. Right now I just need a drink. Anything to make the damn taste of that thing in the mist go away.

ABOUT THE AUTHOR

Annie Reed describes herself as a desert rat who longs to live by the ocean. Born and raised in Northern Nevada, Annie started her writing career in science fiction. She soon branched out to fantasy, mystery, and crime fiction. Annie enjoys character-driven fiction no matter the genre, which is probably why she enjoys such diverse shows as *The Big Bang Theory* and *Sons of Anarchy, Criminal Minds* and *Castle.*

Annie still lives in Northern Nevada with her husband and daughter, who share their house with a number of high-maintenance cats. A friend to back-yard bunnies and kamikaze quail, Annie would probably befriend dogs, too, except they'd chase the rabbits.

To find out more about Annie, visit www.annie-reed.com.

I felt power crackle around the room. I started to say an incantation to create a layer of protection around my mother.

"I wouldn't do that if I were you."

I watched as my mother's face took on a blue tinge, and I realized she wasn't breathing.

"Stop that!" I shouted.

I must have dropped my tea cup. I dimly heard it shatter on the hardwood floor. It was enough to break my concentration, and the spell I had started to cast drifted away from me.

Color returned to my mother's cheeks.

"You've been a bad, bad girl, playing with things beyond your comprehension. I've put a stop to that."

What?

"Who *are* you?"

The air coalesced in front of me. Mist formed into shape, and shape took on substance.

My father's face. The thing in the room with us wore my father's face.

—from "Ties that Bind"